The
Monster
Diner

Written by Mairi Mackinnon

Illustrated by Mike and Carl Gordon

How this book works

The story of **The Monster Diner** has been written for your child to read with your help. Encourage your child to read as much as they can, helping to sound out the words and explaining any meanings if they get stuck.

There are puzzles after the story, and for these you will need to read the instructions to your child.

You can find out more about helping your child with this book, and with reading in general, on pages 30-31.

The Monster Diner

Turn the page to start the story.

"I don't mean to be picky, but that chicken's kind of blue."

"It was fine a month ago.
You say that it won't do?"

"This bread smells dreadful!"

"That cheese is
full of bugs!"

15

"These apricots
are ancient!"

"Those pears are hairy!"

That cake looks scary!

21

"There's a human diner right next door."

Puzzle 1

Match the speech bubbles to the pictures.
(Look back at the story if you need help.)

1. We'd like to order dinner.

2. That chicken's kind of blue.

3. Did you ask to try the salad?

4. That cake looks scary!

5. There's a human diner next door.

Puzzle 2

There is one wrong word in the sentence below each picture. What should they say?

1.

"You say that it won't moo?"

2.

"That cheese is wool
of bugs!"

3.

"Looks like a can of words."

4.

"How cold are those cookies?"

Puzzle 3

Can you find the rhyming pairs? Watch out for the different spellings!

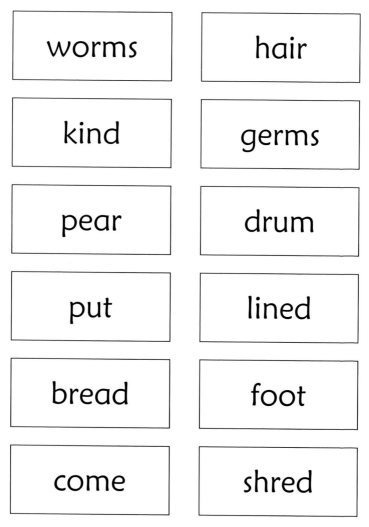

worms

hair

kind

germs

pear

drum

put

lined

bread

foot

come

shred

Answers to puzzles

Puzzle 1

1. "We'd like to order dinner." – E
2. "That chicken's kind of blue." – C
3. "Did you ask to try the salad?" – D
4. "That cake looks scary!" – B
5. "There's a human diner next door." – A

Puzzle 2

1. "You say that it won't <u>do</u>?"
2. "That cheese is <u>full</u> of bugs!"
3. "Looks like a can of <u>worms</u>."
4. "How <u>old</u> are those cookies?"

Puzzle 3

worms — germs
kind — lined
pear — hair
put — foot
bread — shred
come — drum

Guidance notes

Usborne Very First Reading is a series of fifteen books, specially developed for children who are learning to read. **The Monster Diner** is the thirteenth book in the series, and by this stage your child should be able to read the story alone, with occasional help from you.

The story of **The Monster Diner** introduces different ways of pronouncing the letters below:

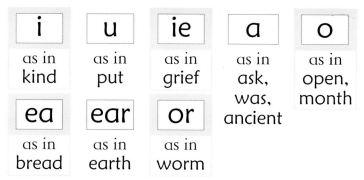

i	u	ie	a	o
as in kind	as in put	as in grief	as in ask, was, ancient	as in open, month

ea	ear	or
as in bread	as in earth	as in worm

Later books in the series look at some more tricky spelling patterns, while reinforcing the patterns your child already knows.

You'll find lots more information about the structure of the series, advice on helping your child with reading, extra practice activities and games on the Usborne Quicklinks website. Just go to **www.usborne-quicklinks.com** and type in the keywords **Very First Reading**.

Some questions and answers

- **Why do I need to read with my child?**
  Sharing stories makes reading an enjoyable and fun activity for children. It also helps them to develop confidence and stamina. Even if you are not taking an active part in reading, your listening and support are very important.

- **When is a good time to read?**
  Choose a time when you are both relaxed, but not too tired, and there are no distractions. Only read for as long as your child wants to – you can always try again another day.

- **What if my child gets stuck?**
  Don't simply read the problem word yourself, but prompt your child and try to find the right answer together. Similarly, if your child makes a mistake, go back and look at the word together. Don't forget to give plenty of praise and encouragement.

- **We've finished, now what do we do?**
  It's a good idea to read the story several times to give your child more practice and more confidence. Then, when your child is ready, you can go on to the next book in the series, **Knight Fight.**

Edited by Jenny Tyler and Lesley Sims
Designed by Russell Punter

First published in 2010 by Usborne Publishing Ltd., Usborne House,
83-85 Saffron Hill, London EC1N 8RT, England. www.usborne.com
Copyright © 2010 Usborne Publishing Ltd.

USBORNE VERY FIRST READING

There are fifteen titles in the **Usborne Very First Reading** series, which has been specially developed to help children learn to read.

To find out more about the structure of the series, go to **www.usborne-quicklinks.com** and type in the keywords **Very First Reading**.

1   2   3

4   5   6